DON'T THROW ANOTHER ONE, DOVER!

BY BEVERLY KELLER
DRAWN BY JACQUELINE CHWAST

Coward, McCann & Geoghegan, Inc.

New York

SBN: GB: 698-30638-4
SBN: TR: 698-20386-0

Library of Congress Cataloging in
Publication Data
Keller, Beverly
Don't throw another one, Dover!
A Break-of-Day Book
Summary: Upset that his mother is going to
have a new baby and that he must stay with
his grandmother, Dover, master of the
tantrum, discovers he's not the only one
who can howl, growl, and kick.
[1. Anger—Fiction.   2. Brothers and
sisters—Fiction.   3. Grandmothers—Fiction]
I. Chwast, Jacqueline.   II. Title.
PZ7.K2813Do   [E]   76-14813

For Justin
Who never . . .
Well, hardly ever. . .
—B.K.

For my brother,
Stanley Weiner
—J.C.

When Dover Beech
went out to play ball,
Dover came right back in.
(He could not throw a ball very well.)

When Dover gave a party,
he invited his friends
and made three kinds of sandwiches.
Nobody had much fun.
(Dover never threw a good party.)

BUT

when Dover's parents told him

he was going to visit

his grandmother,

he threw

the thing he could throw

better than anyone else.

He began to sway
like a mad baboon
till he fell and lay
like a dead balloon.

He howled great long wails
like a wolf pack's call,
while he dug his nails
all along the wall.

When it was over,
his worried mother sighed.
"One thing about Dover—
he throws a great tantrum."

Then she told him
how much she loved him.

"So I get to stay," he said.

But Dover's mother
was going to have a baby
any day.

"Why do you want a baby?"
he asked. "You already have me."

His mother and father
told him again
how they loved him.
"But you still have to go,"
they said.
SO

He fell in a heap,
and he went all pale . . .
which he knew would
be hard to ignore.
He rose with a leap
like a startled whale,
and he battered
his head on the door.

He doubled his fist
till he made it ache
and let out all
his breath in a roar,
then curled up and hissed
like a cornered snake
while he clawed
the fresh wax off the floor.

When he had finished,
his mother and father were pale.
BUT
"You still have to go,
Dover,"
his father said.

Dover was puzzled.
Tantrums had always worked
for him before.

And this had been
one of his best.

"Maybe it needs more work," he decided.
"I'll have to do better

On his way
to his grandmother's house
Dover growled,
"I won't like her."

"You like her every time
you see her," his father
reminded him.

"That's when she
comes to our house,
I won't like her at *her* house."

The minute Dover saw
his grandmother's house,
he knew he didn't like it.

It was tiny
and old
and gray.

His grandmother was on the porch
with a sheep dog
who was
huge and shaggy
and gray.

When his father
kissed him good-bye,
Dover said,
"You're making a big mistake."

He went into the house.

The rugs were faded.
The furniture was worn.
The kitchen stove was black
and stood on curved iron legs.

"Do you want to help
make lunch?"
his grandmother asked.

23

Dover shook his head.
He felt empty.
He sat on the sofa
in the living room
and kicked his heels.

After a while
he went into the kitchen.
"Is there any ice cream
in the freezer?"

"I don't have a freezer,"
his grandmother said.
"But maybe later
we can make ice cream."

Dover wondered how anybody
without a freezer
could make ice cream.
"Where's your television?"

"I don't have a set."

Dover wondered how anybody
could live without television.

When his grandmother put lunch
on the table, he said,
"I'm not hungry."

But
lunch was
baked macaroni
with bubbly cheese,
corn on the cob,
and hot rolls with butter
and honey.

Dover pretended
he was only eating to be polite.

After lunch he took his plate
to the sink. "Where's your
dishwasher machine?"

"I don't have one."

"Boy." Dover shook his head.
He didn't even ask where
her garbage machine was.
He could see
that his grandmother
didn't have much of anything.

When the dishes were done,
he followed her upstairs.

"Would you like to see
pictures of your father
when he was a baby?" she asked.

Dover did not want
to think about babies.
He shook his head.

"Would you like to play checkers?"

"I want to go home," he said.

"How would you like
to make popcorn?"

"I want to go *home!*"

"I know you do,"
his grandmother said.
"After your mother has the baby,
you can."

"I WANT TO GO NOW!"

"Well, you can't."

He turned red.
He turned blue. He turned white.
The dog fled.
The moths flew from the sight.

First he fell downstairs
to command attention.
Then he moved her chairs
for his next invention.

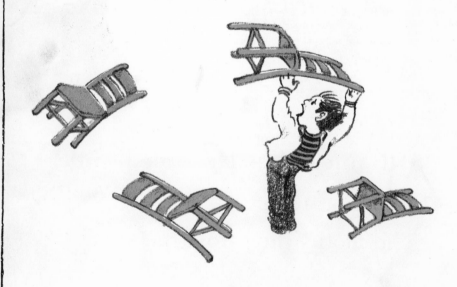

Like a dinosaur
rising from some tar pit,
he scratched up her floor;
then he bit her carpet.

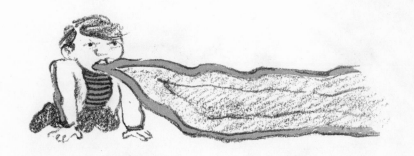

He heard her coming
down the stairs.
He heard her voice, above him.
"A good tantrum," she said,
"but not a great one."
SO

He filled up his lungs
with one great inhaling,
then he tore the rungs
from her staircase railing!

He let out that air
with a roar so horrid,
that it raised the hair
on the sheep dog's forehead.

His grandmother
stepped over him.

He thought maybe she had gone
for the police
or an ambulance.

Then from outside came a growl
and a terrible howl
and a hair-raising yowl.

He ran to the back door.

His grandmother was under a tree
jumping up and down,
showing her teeth,
and shaking her fists.

Dover trembled.

He wondered if he should

call the police

or an ambulance.

Then she strolled

away from the tree.

Dover wandered outside.
He pretended
he was just looking around.

The dog, whose name was Heloise,
saw him coming
and walked the other way.

Dover watched his grandmother
while she fed chickens and ducks
and picked berries
and petted a big, beautiful cow.
She seemed to be over her tantrum.
Still, Dover did not get too close.

When she went back to the house,
he sat by a pond
and wondered
what would happen if he fell in.

From the kitchen
came a pounding.

He ran to see
what was happening.

His grandmother was on her knees
hitting the floor with a hammer.

Dover watched
with his heart pounding his ribs.

He had never imagined
throwing a tantrum with a hammer!

She gave the floor
another awful bang.
After she stood,
she jumped up and down again!
Then she left the room.

Dover
heard a crash.

He thought
maybe
his grandmother was
falling down the cellar stairs.

He ran to see.

She was at the bottom
of the steps
kicking at the cellar door.

Dover decided
this time
she was throwing
the greatest tantrum in the world.

She kicked and kicked
and kicked that door.
It shivered.
It shuddered.
Dover shook.

The door flew open.
Dover's grandmother
walked through the doorway
into the cellar.

Dover stood at the top of the stairs
with his hand over his mouth.
When she came out carrying a jar,
he backed all the way
to the kitchen.
"Set the table for tea,"
she said.

46

For tea,
they had
jam on fresh bread,
strawberries from the garden,
and milk from the beautiful cow.

But Dover couldn't eat.
"Grandma," he whispered at last,
"why did you stamp and yell
and shake your fist at the tree?"

"There was a cat in the tree
going after a bird's nest.
I shooed him away."
She plopped a big spoonful
of jam on his bread.

"Why were you hitting
your floor with a hammer?"

She piled strawberries on his plate.
"I was nailing down a loose board."

"Why did you kick
your door so hard?"

"It sticks, but we can fix it."

Dover dunked
a strawberry in his milk.

After tea he and his grandmother
fixed the cellar door
so it opened without being kicked.

Then Heloise brought him a stick.
She chased it even when he didn't
throw it very well.

That evening
Dover and his grandmother
were making ice cream
when the telephone rang.

Dover answered it.

"You have a new baby sister,"
his father told him.

"I have to crank
the ice-cream machine,"
Dover said.

He handed the telephone
to his grandmother.

When his father came to get him,
Dover said, "I won't go."

He took in a breath
and let out a moan . . . .

"You only get one,"
his grandmother said.

He doubled his fists
and began to groan . . . .

"You've thrown one tantrum
in my house," she said.
"If you're going to throw
another,
you have to throw it
where you won't bother me
or my animals."

Dover scowled at her.
She looked at him.
He remembered
how she could howl
and growl
and stamp,
and shake her fist,
and hammer the floor,
and jump up and down,
and kick the door.

And he knew
that tantrums
would never be the same for him.
Not when his grandmother
could stomp and yell
and pound and kick and jump
without even throwing one.

Besides,
a tantrum is not really a tantrum
when there's no one around
to admire it.

"All right," he said.
"I have to throw
the ducks and chickens
some feed.
Then I'll throw the cow some hay.
I'll throw
one more stick for Heloise.
Then I'll throw my clothes
in a suitcase."

When he got home,
he let his mother kiss him.
"Would you like to see your sister?"
she asked.

"Not much."

But he helped
his mother give her a bath.
He washed her toes,
which were very small.
He dried her fingers,
which curled around his thumb.

Then he went outside
and found his friends.
He told them how to fix doors
and nail floors
and promised to let them
come see his new sister.

He went to bed without fussing.
His father had to
tell him good-night
only three times.

He thought maybe
he would take the baby with him
the next time
he went to his grandmother's.
He had a lot to teach his sister
about saving birds
and making ice cream
and throwing sticks
and tantrums.

About the Author

Beverly Keller has been adopted by lots of stray dogs and cats near her home in Davis, California. She loves plants, making collages, refinishing furniture, and being involved in "all sorts of messy projects."

The author began writing when she was about eight or ten, collaborating on a newspaper with her friend Florence. She went on to write newspaper columns and magazine stories and an espionage novel, *The Baghdad Defections*.

Beverly Keller's first book for children, *Fiona's Bee*, was starred by *Kirkus Reviews*, which called it "the bee's knees." Her second book for children, *The Beetle Bush*, is all about success and failure.

About the Artist

Jacqueline Chwast's special illustrations have appeared in such children's books as *I Like Old Clothes, Picnics and Parades, Sing Song Scuppernong,* and *Aunt Bella's Umbrella*. The artist also contributes to such magazines as *New York, Harper's, MS.,* and *Scholastic*.

A graduate of the Newark School of Fine and Industrial Arts, Jacqueline Chwast lives in New York City with her two daughters, Eve and Pamela.